JEFF SZPIRGLAS

ILLUSTRATED BY
DAVE WHAMOND

ORCA BOOK PUBLISHERS

Library and Archives Canada Cataloguing in Publication

Szpirglas, Jeff, author
Wild cards / Jeff Szpirglas ; illustrated by Dave Whamond.
(Orca echoes)

Issued in print and electronic formats.
ISBN 978-1-4598-1211-6 (paperback).—ISBN 978-1-4598-1212-3 (pdf).—
ISBN 978-1-4598-1213-0 (epub)

I. Whamond, Dave, illustrator II. Title. III. Series: Orca echoes
PS8637.Z654W54 2017   jc813'.6   C2016-904472-6
C2016-904473-4

First published in the United States, 2017
Library of Congress Control Number: 2016950086

Summary: In this illustrated early chapter book, a game of trading playing cards gets
out of hand at a grade school with big problems.

Orca Book Publishers gratefully acknowledges the support for its publishing programs
provided by the following agencies: the Government of Canada through the Canada Book Fund
and the Canada Council for the Arts, and the Province of British Columbia
through the BC Arts Council and the Book Publishing Tax Credit.

MIX
Paper from
responsible sources
FSC® C103567

*Orca Book Publishers is dedicated to preserving the environment and has printed
this book on Forest Stewardship Council® certified paper.*

Cover artwork and interior illustrations by Dave Whamond
Author photo by Tim Basile

ORCA BOOK PUBLISHERS
www.orcabook.com

Printed and bound in Canada.

20 19 18 17 • 4 3 2 1

For Léo and Ruby

CHAPTER ONE

Matt loved *Monster Zap* cards.

Matt also loved the *Monster Zap* TV show and playing the *Monster Zap* video game after school. He had *Monster Zap* toys and *Monster Zap* graphic novels, and he slept in *Monster Zap* pajamas.

He even had *Monster Zap* underwear.

Matt had over fifty *Monster Zap* cards. They had pictures of monsters on the front, with facts about their skills and powers on the back. You used the cards to play a game with your friends that challenged their *Monster Zap* cards. You pulled cards from your deck to see if your skill points could beat the skill points on somebody else's monster cards. If someone else had better skill points, they took *your* points away. Whoever had the most points after a round of play won. That meant you traded your good cards away to the winner.

The cards came in packs of five and cost three dollars each. Some cards turned up in packs more than others. Matt already had five Blobazoids and three Duck Slimes. Other cards were harder to find. They only turned up in packages once in a while.

Matt had one card that was super special.

It was printed on gold-colored foil paper. It was a Blue-Fanged Gobbler. When Matt played *Monster Zap* with his friends, he kept his Blue-Fanged Gobbler close by. It could take the most points away from any other card if he pulled it out of the deck during a game.

On Tuesday, Matt put the Gobbler in a plastic card case and gently slipped it into his backpack. He took it with him to school. At morning recess, he took it out.

There was not a lot to do at recess besides play with *Monster Zap* cards. The play area outside the school was just flat, hard concrete.

It was also really gross out there. The schoolyard was covered with garbage. Crumpled bags, plastic wrap and even crusts from bread. Nobody ever put their trash in the garbage cans. Kids just threw their junk on the pavement.

Plus, there was no jungle gym like the one at the park down the street. There were only a few balls, skipping ropes and Hula-Hoops to use. Most of the big kids took those. And it had been a wet spring, so the field was too muddy to play on.

At least Matt had his cards.

When Matt's friend Tyler saw the Blue-Fanged Gobbler, he put his hands on his head and said, *"Eeearrrgh!"*

"Are you okay?" Matt said.

Tyler jumped up and down twelve times. *"Eeearrrgh!* That's a Blue-Fanged Gobbler, Matt!" He jumped up and down some more.

"I know."

"That's the best card I've ever seen!" Tyler kept jumping.

Matt nodded. "Me too."

"Did you say a Blue-Fanged Gobbler?" another voice called out.

Before Matt knew it, five or six other kids were gathered around him and Tyler.

"Whoa!"

"That card rules!"

Soon they all had their cards out and were happily playing *Monster Zap*. Not long after they started, it was time to trade.

Matt would never trade his Blue-Fanged Gobbler. But he did have a Fire-Breathing Zwart, which was a pretty good card. Tyler saw it, and his eyes grew as big as saucers.

"Whoa! I want that Zwart!" Tyler said.

Matt looked at the Zwart card in his hand. He stared at the Gross Eyeball card in Tyler's hand. "I'll trade you the Zwart for the Eyeball."

Tyler looked at his card. "My uncle bought me this one. He got it from a special card shop." Tyler gave the Eyeball card a long stare. He took a deep breath. He *really* wanted that Zwart. "Okay," he said finally.

Slowly Tyler handed the Eyeball card to Matt. Matt gave him the Zwart.

Matt smiled. He needed a Gross Eyeball for his collection.

"Wait," Tyler said. "Give that back. I changed my mind."

Matt shook his head. "No. You traded it fair and square."

Tyler stepped closer to Matt. "I want my Gross Eyeball back. Come on."

Matt tried to put the card in his pocket. "You said you wanted to trade it."

Tyler reached forward to grab it out of Matt's hand, but Matt was too quick. Tyler missed and fell to the pavement.

"Whoa!" some of the kids around them said.

"*Whoa* is right," came another voice.

Everyone turned.

It was Mr. Leon, the school principal. He was out on recess duty. His face was the same color as the red shirt he was wearing.

Matt gulped. This meant big trouble.

CHAPTER TWO

In a flash, all of the other kids ran away. "Wait!" Mr. Leon said, but he was too late. Only Matt and Tyler were left. Mr. Leon turned to them. "Why are you fighting?"

Tyler shook his head. "It's not a fight. It's a..."

"It's a mistake," Matt said. He reached into his pocket. "I'm sorry, Tyler. You can have your Gross Eyeball back."

"Thanks, Matt." Tyler moved to take the card from Matt, but Mr. Leon stopped him.

"What is *that*?"

"It's a Gross Eyeball, Mr. Leon."

Mr. Leon's eyeballs grew so big that they looked gross too. "Are those *Monster Zap* cards?"

Tyler looked at Matt. "Uh, maybe?"

Mr. Leon took a deep breath. "There are too many fights over these *Monster Zap* cards."

"It's not a fight," Matt said. He could see that Mr. Leon was upset. Matt took Tyler's hand and shook it. "See? We're friends again." He smiled a big smile.

Tyler saw what Matt was doing and gave a big smile too. "Friends forever, Matt! Problem solved!" Tyler said as he continued to shake Matt's hand.

"Too many fights, boys. Those cards are causing too many issues. Give them to me, please."

"But…"

Mr. Leon held out his hand. "You can have them at the end of the day. They will be in my office."

Matt gulped.

"But what else are we supposed to do at recess?" Tyler asked. "The field is too wet to play on. There aren't enough soccer balls to use. It's *boring* out here."

Mr. Leon looked at the schoolyard. "Why don't you play tag? Or hide-and-seek?"

Matt and Tyler looked at each other. "There's nowhere to hide, Mr. Leon," Matt said.

Mr. Leon shrugged. "I'm sure you will figure it out. Now please give me those cards."

Tyler handed over his stack. So did Matt.

"I'll see you at the end of the day," Mr. Leon said. Then he looked past the boys. Two girls were standing up to their ankles in mud on the wet soccer field. "Oh no! Another problem. Girls, put those mud pies down!!!" Mr. Leon left Tyler and Matt in a hurry.

There sure were a lot of problems outside at recess.

"Great," Tyler said. "Now Mr. Leon's got our cards. What are we going to do?"

Matt shrugged. "Go and play?"

The recess bell rang.

Tyler grumbled. "*Urgh*. I can't wait

until three o'clock. I want those cards
back now."

Matt spent the rest of the day trying to
listen to his teacher, Miss Casey. But he
was really counting the minutes until he
could get his Gobbler back. Just before
the final bell rang, the school loudspeaker came on.

"Attention, students," Mr. Leon's
voice boomed. "There have been many
problems at recess and in class with
students trading *Monster Zap* cards.
Because we are having trouble finding
a solution, *Monster Zap* cards will be
banned, starting tomorrow. Thank you for
your help, and have a great afternoon."

The loudspeaker went off.

"Did you hear that?" Tyler shouted. "*Monster Zap* cards are banned. That's great news!" Tyler looked at Miss Casey and the rest of the class. "Isn't it?"

Miss Casey shook her head. "No, Tyler. *Banned* means that *Monster Zap* cards are not allowed at school anymore."

Tyler and Matt stared at each other in disbelief.

CHAPTER THREE

After the final school bell, Matt and Tyler dashed down to the office.

Matt had never been to Mr. Leon's office before. He was a bit afraid.

"Don't worry," Tyler said. "I don't think we're in trouble."

"Come in, boys," they heard Mr. Leon say.

Matt and Tyler entered the office. There were pictures on the wall of

Mr. Leon and his family. Mr. Leon had two sons a bit older than Matt and Tyler. There were also pictures on the wall of comic-book heroes. Mr. Leon even had a huge framed superhero poster on his wall. It showed a superhero in a green suit and red cape with a mask over his face.

"Wow!" Tyler said. "Is that Powerman?"

Mr. Leon nodded. "I got that when I was your age."

"It's probably worth a lot," Matt said. "Maybe even as much as my Blue-Fanged Gobbler." Then Matt saw the pile of cards on Mr. Leon's desk. "Can I have my cards back now?"

"Yes," Mr. Leon said, "but they can't come to school anymore."

"Why are you banning the cards?" Matt asked.

Mr. Leon took a deep breath. "You know, boys, they banned Powerman at my school when I was a kid. And other comic books too. People thought comics were bad to read. My teacher used to take them from me and send them home in my backpack."

Matt looked at the poster of Powerman on Mr. Leon's wall. "There's a graphic-novel section in our library."

"There never used to be," Mr. Leon said. "I'm glad there is. I still love Powerman. Those comics helped me learn to read. I know they are helping other kids learn to read too. That's why we keep them here in the school." Mr. Leon looked at the *Monster Zap* cards on his desk. "I know you love these *Monster Zap* cards like I love comics. I don't want to keep these cards from coming to school,"

Mr. Leon said. "But people have already gotten hurt, and I don't want that happening to anyone else. Do you?"

Matt thought about this. "The school has lots of problems besides cards," he said. "Sometimes people play too rough at other games. But we don't ban those games. And there's not much to do. The yard is full of garbage."

"Yeah," Tyler said. "Are the caretakers dumping the garbage cans in the schoolyard?"

"No," Mr. Leon said.

"Plus," Tyler said, "they never *return* anything. I had this great super-bouncy ball once, but I bounced it too hard, and it's up on the roof of the school now. I probably have at least six bouncy balls up there. Do you think the caretakers play games up there with our stuff?"

Mr. Leon stared at the boys. "This sounds like a big problem, and we need to find a solution. Can you think of one?"

Matt didn't have an answer. Not yet.

CHAPTER FOUR

After he finished his homework, Matt wanted to watch the *Monster Zap* TV show. But his big sister, Becky, was already watching some other show about teenagers. "You had your turn yesterday," she told him.

Matt grumbled. He couldn't have *Monster Zap* at school, and now he couldn't have it at home either.

Or could he?

Matt went to his room. He took out some paper and pencil crayons.

Then Matt started to draw. He looked at his Blue-Fanged Gobbler card. It wasn't too hard to draw. He made sure to add the sharp blue teeth and hairy fur. His drawing looked almost the same as the one on the card.

Matt smiled.

It wasn't just a good picture. Now he had a good *idea* too.

The next morning, Matt met up with Tyler by the fence outside the school. Tyler was angry. "Can you believe it, Matt? No *Monster Zap*. I stared at my own cards this morning for half an hour. I know the numbers on those cards better than the numbers we are supposed to know for our math quiz! Go ahead. Try me."

"What's three plus six?"

"I have no idea. But did you know that a Hog-Snouted Blugger has nine skill points?"

"Did you know that three plus six is *also* nine?" said Matt.

"Wow, *Monster Zap* cards have *everything*. Even the answers to math questions. Too bad we can't use them at school anymore."

Matt dug into his pocket. He pulled out a folded piece of paper. "But we can use this…"

He unfolded the paper.

Tyler's eyes grew as big as basketballs. "That's your Blue-Fanged Gobbler! That's a great picture."

"Thanks," Matt said. He showed the other side to Tyler. "I copied down the facts from my card at home. See?"

"But *Monster Zap* is banned, remember?"

Matt shook his head. "*Monster Zap cards* are banned. I made this one myself." He reached into his other pocket and took out another few drawings he had stuffed in there. "I also made some other drawings."

"Matt," Tyler said, "you are a genius!"

"Whoa! What's that?" said another voice.

"Matt's got *Monster Zap!*" Tyler shouted.

"Tyler, stop shouting," Matt said.

"Sorry!" Tyler shouted. "I get very excited about *Monster Zap!*"

Soon a bunch of kids were gathered around Matt and Tyler. Steve and Mark were the closest. They tried to push and shove their way even closer to Matt to see the drawings. "Come on, Matt. Show us your cards!"

Matt felt the boys start bumping into him. "They're not cards," Matt said. "Just pictures I drew."

Steve and Mark and the other boys were too close. Matt started to put the drawings back into his pocket. But Mark bumped into him, and he began to lose his balance. "Watch out—I'm going to fall!"

"Me too!" Steve said.

One by one, the boys knocked each other over like bowling pins.

"What is going on here?"

Matt looked up from the pile of boys to see a figure standing over them. "Uh, hi, Miss Casey."

"What are you doing?" she asked.

Tyler pulled himself out of the pile. "We were just doing…uh…some yoga stretches."

"That's right," Mark said.

"I live for yoga!" Steve said.

Miss Casey gave the boys a long look. Matt wondered if she could see the *Monster Zap* pictures in his pocket. Were his drawings causing a problem too?

"Well," Miss Casey said, "whatever you are doing, be safe." She moved on to watch another part of the schoolyard.

"Phew, that was close," Steve said.

Mark looked at Matt. "But you gave me a good idea. We can make our own *Monster Zap* cards!"

Then Mark looked at Steve. "I know what kinds of monsters we can put on them."

The two boys laughed. Matt knew that laugh. It was an *up-to-no-good* kind of laugh.

CHAPTER FIVE

Miss Casey always started her class at reading and writing centers while she worked with small groups. Today, Matt chose the writing center at the far end of the room.

Miss Casey was not like other teachers. She had a pet spider and drove a motorcycle to school. She liked scary movies and heavy metal music. She said it was okay if students made drawings to go with their writing.

The *Monster Zap* cards were full of writing. Matt chose to make up facts for his new monsters and turn them into cards.

Matt opened up his writing notebook and began to draw monster pictures. He made up new monsters that lived in his mind. One of his monsters had long scaly arms that dragged behind it. Another had teeth made from pencils. Matt wrote a sentence about each monster.

"Matt?"

Matt was still hunched over the desk, writing.

"Matt, can you come to the carpet, please?"

Matt looked up. The rest of the class was sitting on the carpet. So was Miss Casey. They were looking right at him.

"What are you making, Matt?" Miss Casey asked.

Matt looked down at his notebook. He put his hand over the work.

But already Victoria was on her feet. "They're *Monster Zap* cards!" she screamed. "They are not allowed. Mr. Leon said they are *banned*."

Matt stood up and shook his head. "Mr. Leon did not want cards coming to school. But these are not cards. These are my own." Matt passed his work over to Miss Casey.

Soon everyone was crowded around Miss Casey. They were trying to get a look at Matt's work.

"Are they allowed, Miss Casey?" asked Emily.

"Matt's cards show a lot of skill," Miss Casey said. "He has labeled the pictures. He has used full sentences about each monster on the back." She handed Matt his notebook. "I think you've done a great job, Matt."

Matt smiled.

Victoria raised her hand. "Can we make *Monster Zap* cards too, Miss Casey?"

Miss Casey stared at the class. Everyone had leaned in close, waiting for her answer.

"Sure," she said. "But let's make some rules first. We can make them as long as they are respectful. We can put them up on the wall so everyone can look at them."

The class burst into cheers.

"Also," Miss Casey said, "make sure you describe your monsters using full sentences."

There were not as many cheers *that* time.

Miss Casey put a finger to her chin, which she did when she was thinking about something. "Maybe we shouldn't call them *Monster Zap* cards," she said. "That way it will be very clear to Mr. Leon that these are not the same thing."

"I know!" Tyler said. "We can call them Monster Barf cards!"

"Uh...let's call them Monster Fun cards," Miss Casey said.

Before Matt knew it, everybody in the class was making monster cards. He took a break from his own cards and walked around the room. He could see pictures of big monsters, small monsters and weird monsters.

Miss Casey came up beside Matt. "This is going quite well," she said. "Everyone is drawing. Everyone is writing. Matt, your idea really inspired the other students. Good job."

"Thanks, Miss Casey."

"You can be quite a leader when you want to be," she added.

Matt had never *inspired* anyone before. It felt good.

When it was time to have snacks, Matt made sure to eat over his desk, like Miss Casey asked. He made sure to put his garbage in the bin. And he made sure to put his indoor shoes side by side before putting on his outdoor shoes for recess.

When the recess bell rang, Matt didn't run down the hall like Tyler did. He walked carefully. He knew Miss Casey was watching him.

"Come on, Matt!" Tyler yelled from the doorway at the far end of the hall. "What's the holdup?"

Matt was about to say something when Steve and Mark came pushing by. They were giggling and laughing. They had a bunch of papers in their hands. Matt could tell they were hand-drawn monster pictures.

But they weren't pictures of monsters.

Matt got a closer look at the pictures Steve and Mark had drawn.

They were pictures of Mr. Leon!

CHAPTER SIX

All of that good feeling inside Matt drained away.

Matt's heart began to thud in his chest like a giant drum. His head felt dizzy. What would happen if Mr. Leon found those pictures?

He had to stop Mark and Steve!

Matt ran across the schoolyard after them. A big crowd was already growing around them. Some were kids his own age.

But there was also a group of older kids passing Mark's and Steve's papers around. They looked at the pictures and burst out laughing.

Mark saw Matt coming over. "Hi, Matt. Do you want a picture? I couldn't have made them without your great idea!"

He passed one of the pictures to Matt.

It was a picture of Mr. Leon, but he had fangs instead of his regular smile. He had hairy ears and big jagged lines shooting out of his nostrils. "What are those?" Matt said.

"Oh, those? That's Mr. Leon's superpower," Mark said. "He can shoot ultra boogers from his nose!"

Other kids started to laugh.

Matt's throat felt tight. Maybe this would have been funny if they were drawings of a fake person, but not Mr. Leon.

"I can shoot ultra boogers from my nose too," Steve said. "Watch!"

Before Steve could do anything gross, Matt grabbed the handful of pictures from Mark's hand and ran.

"Get back here! Those pictures took at least five minutes to draw!"

Matt clutched the pictures close to his chest. He had to make sure Mr. Leon didn't see them. He rounded a corner of the school and—

POW!

Matt ran right into something.

He fell flat on the pavement with a loud thud and dropped all the pictures.

Matt tried taking deep breaths. His head was still spinning. He looked in front of him. What had he run into?

"Ouch, Matt! I know we like playing together, but this is too much!"

Phew! It was Tyler.

"You've got to help me," Matt said. He pointed to the papers scattered around them.

"Wow, Matt. You were really busy making cards!"

"They're not mine," Matt said.

Tyler looked more closely at the cards. "Did you make those about Mr. Leon? That's...kind of mean, Matt."

Matt shook his head. "It was Mark and Steve. They will get everyone into trouble. We have to get rid of these *now*!"

Matt tried to grab the pictures, but a big wind blew across the schoolyard. It tossed the papers around the boys. Tyler started to grab some.

Matt jumped to his feet. One of the papers was being flung around by the wind. Matt ran after it. The paper swirled and swooped. Matt reached out with his hand. He almost had it. Just a few feet more...

The paper flew into someone's face. An *adult's* face.

Matt stopped.

He watched as the person pulled the paper away from his face.

Matt groaned.

It was Mr. Leon.

CHAPTER SEVEN

"What's this?" Mr. Leon said.

Matt gulped. "Uh…"

Maybe Mr. Leon wouldn't notice it was a picture of him. Then Matt saw how red Mr. Leon's face was getting.

"This is a *Monster Zap* card," Mr. Leon said. "Of me!"

Matt tried to talk, but his mouth just hung open.

Mr. Leon narrowed his eyes. "Are those stink lines?"

Matt shook his head. "It's not mine. I didn't make it!"

Then Matt explained everything that had happened that morning. Mr. Leon listened.

"I understand," Mr. Leon said at last. He did not look angry with Matt, but he did not look happy either. "Here's how you can help. Go and find the rest of these pictures. You can put them in the recycling bin."

"All of them? Or just the ones by Mark and Steve?"

"Matt, you have good ideas. But this one is getting out of hand. I think I know how to solve this problem."

"Okay," Matt said. That made him feel a bit better. Matt turned away from Mr. Leon and went looking for the other pictures.

Still, Matt was not sure how Mr. Leon was going to stop people from making their own cards.

After recess, it was time for math.

Miss Casey had already stapled a few of the Monster Fun pictures to the bulletin board outside the classroom. Matt saw Victoria and her friend Emily pointing and looking at them.

"Will you draw me one of those Bearded Boogers?" Victoria asked Emily.

Emily nodded. "Sure. I bet Miss Casey will give us some extra time after math."

Matt smiled. It was nice to know that not everybody got into fights over trading cards.

Tyler came up to Matt. "I saw you with Mr. Leon. Are you in big trouble?"

Matt shook his head. "He said he had a solution to the problem."

Tyler looked around. "But besides Steve's and Mark's cards, there is no problem."

"I know," Matt said. "But does Mr. Leon?"

Matt and Tyler went into the classroom. They stopped when they saw what was drawn on the board.

"It's a Blue-Fanged Gobbler!" Tyler yelled. "Just like your card, Matt!"

Miss Casey stood by the board. "You really like shouting, Tyler."

Tyler shrugged. "I can't help it! That's what happens when you put me near *Monster Zap*!"

Soon the rest of the class was crowded around the board too. "Wow,

that's a great picture, Miss Casey. Are we doing *Monster Zap* for math?"

Miss Casey had all of the students sit down on the carpet. "Boys and girls, I am glad you like my drawing. But did you see the words beside it?"

Matt noticed there was a math problem on the board too.

The class read it together. "*If the Blue-Fanged Gobbler has 17 skill points, and if a Zwart takes away 9 skill points, how many does it have left?*"

Tyler never answered math questions, but now he was counting on his fingers. He raised his hand.

"Yes, Tyler?"

"That's easy! There are 8 skill points left."

Miss Casey smiled. "It looks like you are good at solving math problems, Tyler."

Tyler's face went red. Math was not his strength. "Really?"

Then the loudspeaker crackled to life. "Attention, students. This is Mr. Leon. It has been brought to my attention that some students have been making new monster cards and trading them at recess. Not all of them are respectful. I am asking students not to trade any kind of card at recess. Even ones made by students. Thank you, and have a good day."

The room was silent.

Matt shook his head. "*That's* Mr. Leon's solution? I can't believe it!"

CHAPTER EIGHT

Tyler folded his arms across his chest. "No drawing monsters? That's like no eating or drinking."

Victoria raised her hand to speak. "You'd better get rid of that picture of the Gobbler before Mr. Leon sees it."

Miss Casey sighed. "Boys and girls, let's talk about this." She looked at the circle of students. "I see that Mr. Leon has made a rule you do not agree with."

Tyler jumped to his feet. "It's a crazy rule!" he said. "Kids have food fights all the time, and they don't ban lunch."

"I know," Matt said. "Only a few people had problems with cards at recess. Most kids can trade them without getting into fights."

When Matt saw how well the class was listening, it made him feel good. Even if he still felt angry about the rule. "Plus," Matt said, "*Monster Zap* helped with math. Tyler solved that problem about the Blue-Fanged Gobbler."

Tyler, who was still standing, pointed at the board. "He's right. Those Gobblers have amazing powers!"

"Thank you, Tyler," Miss Casey said. "I think you can sit down now." She looked at the class. "It sounds like you have good reasons to keep

Monster Zap. Or, at least, Monster Fun. What should we do about it?"

Victoria raised her hand. "*You* should tell Mr. Leon to change the rule."

"But I don't collect *Monster Zap* cards," Miss Casey said.

"I know!" Emily said. "We can write him a letter. We'll get all of the students to sign it. Not just in our class, but in other classes too."

Matt nodded. "That's a good idea. Mr. Leon wants to see us working together. But it's not enough."

"Why not?" Emily asked.

"I don't think he trusts us at recess. Even if there weren't *Monster Zap* cards, there would be something else he'd get upset with. But the cards aren't the real problem." Matt looked past the students, out the window. He stared at the empty playground. He watched the wind toss a plastic bag and twirl it through the air. Matt looked back at the class. "There's not enough to do at recess time. That's why kids keep having fights and stuff."

"You're right! Kids act totally wild out there," Tyler said. "*Monster Zap* cards give us something to do, but with all the fights we might as well call them 'Kids-Go-Wild Cards!'"

"There aren't any more balls and skipping ropes at the office for us to use," said Emily.

"And the lines for hopscotch have faded off the pavement," Victoria added.

Miss Casey sat there and listened as students shared their concerns. "This sounds like a super problem," she said.

A *super* problem.

Matt's eyes went wide.

He opened his mouth and gasped.

"Matt, are you okay?" Tyler asked. "Did you swallow a bug or something?"

Matt jumped to his feet. "Miss Casey is right!" he said. "It *is* a super problem. And it needs a *super* solution!"

Then Matt told the class his idea. Everyone, even Miss Casey, listened. "What do you think?"

"It's going to take a lot of work," Miss Casey said. "And a lot of leadership. We'll have to convince Mr. Leon. He might say no."

"I know," Matt said.

For the rest of the morning, the class worked on the idea. They wrote their letter. They picked their jobs.

Miss Casey had planned on teaching other subjects that day. But the class used their art period to work on solving the problem. And their social studies period too!

Matt and Tyler even stayed in at lunchtime to help Miss Casey organize the materials. They needed towels. They needed safety pins. They needed lots of construction paper. Matt and Tyler helped cut out the shapes the class would need.

Miss Casey came by and looked at their work. "Tyler and Matt, I am really impressed by what good leaders you are being," she told them.

"Really?" Tyler said. "Because last week you kept me in at recess for throwing papers around."

Miss Casey smiled. "You needed to stay and clean up. But today you chose to stay and help."

There was a knock at the door.

Matt looked up from his work. "Mr. Leon!" he said.

Tyler shook his head. "You *can't* be here!"

"I can't? But I'm the principal."

"But you'll ruin the surprise!"

Mr. Leon blinked. "Surprise?"

Miss Casey smiled. "Tyler wants to show you our plan."

Mr. Leon looked around the room. "What's the plan?"

Then Matt and Tyler told Mr. Leon about their idea. They were worried he wouldn't like it. "What do you think?" Matt said.

Mr. Leon looked at Matt and Tyler and all of their work in the classroom. Finally, he took a deep breath. "Boys, I think Miss Casey is right."

"What do you mean?"

"I think you two are excellent leaders. And I like your solution even better than mine."

"You do?"

"Yes," Mr. Leon said. "And Tyler is also right. I think your class needs to keep this a big surprise. We will put on your presentation for the whole school tomorrow."

CHAPTER NINE

There was a lot to do.

Matt got to school extra early to help Miss Casey. Other students in his class did too. They pulled out some mats from the gym and put them in the schoolyard.

Matt was just about to grab some other gear they'd need when Mark and Steve came walking up to him. They did not look happy.

"Mr. Leon called our parents," Mark said. "My mom said I can't play *Monster Zap* on the computer for a week!"

"This was all *your* idea," Steve grumbled.

Matt shook his head. "I made monster cards. You made ones that made fun of Mr. Leon and the teachers. That wasn't my idea."

Then Steve saw something at the far edge of the schoolyard, by the back fence. "Hey, what's that?" He pointed across the field. Miss Casey was standing on a big gym mat. A bunch of other mats were lying around it. Miss Casey was talking into a big megaphone. A crowd of students was already gathering around her.

"Isn't that Miss Casey?" Mark said to Matt.

But Matt just smiled. The plan was working. Except...where was Mr. Leon?

"Let's get closer," Steve said. "I can't hear!"

Matt followed them over to where Miss Casey was. He looked around for Mr. Leon. He should have been there already.

"Boys and girls," Miss Casey started, "I know our schoolyard has big problems. You might even say we have *super* problems. And super problems need super solutions. So...I give you the Super Squad!"

Miss Casey stepped aside. Behind her stood the other kids from Matt's class. They were all wearing T-shirts with the letter *S* pinned to them, and they wore towels around their necks like capes.

Victoria and Emily started to skip with jump ropes on the mats.

Miss Casey lowered the megaphone for Victoria. "We're the Skipping Squad," Victoria said. "We're going to be doing a skip-rope station every morning recess by the hopscotch pad."

"And the hopscotch pad will be painted by our Tarmac Crew," Miss Casey added. She pointed to a few more of Matt's classmates.

Then a few other students came to the front of the mats. Miss Casey pointed to them. "These will be our new Door Monitors. They'll keep the hallways safe at recess."

"And now," Miss Casey said, "our Waste Busters!"

"*What*?" Steve said.

"That's me!" Matt said. He ran over to where Miss Casey was. Tyler was already standing there, holding the megaphone.

"Yeah," Tyler added. "Every recess we're going to help clean up around the school—in the classrooms and outside on the schoolyard."

Everyone around Tyler cheered.

Everyone but Matt.

"What's wrong?" Tyler whispered.

"Where's Mr. Leon? He said he would be here."

Miss Casey took the megaphone. "Don't worry," she whispered to Matt and Tyler. Then she pointed past the crowd. "And don't forget Captain Cleanup!"

"Who?" Matt asked.

"That's me!" boomed a voice from behind them.

Everyone in the crowd turned. Behind them stood a man dressed in a green, tight-fitting, superhero suit. He had a red cape, a thick belt with lots of pockets and a big buckle, and a mask around his eyes. He flexed his muscles.

"Mr. Leon!" Matt cried.

This was not part of the plan.

CHAPTER TEN

Mr. Leon was dressed exactly like the Powerman poster in his office.

"Mr. Leon?" some of the other kids asked.

Mr. Leon marched over to Miss Casey and took the megaphone from her. "Mr. Leon? Who's *he*? I'm Captain Cleanup!"

The students laughed.

"This schoolyard is a mess. It needs superheroes like Captain Cleanup and the Super Squad."

Mr. Leon opened one of the pockets on his belt and pulled out some papers.

Matt couldn't believe it. "Are those *Monster Zap* cards?"

"Not *Monster Zap* cards. These are superhero cards." Mr. Leon started passing them out to the students.

Tyler took one and looked at it. "But they're blank, Mr. Leon...er... Captain Cleanup. There's nothing on them."

"That's right," Mr. Leon said. "I want you to draw *yourself* as a superhero. Or a monster. Or whatever you like. Anyone can be a Captain Cleanup and help clean up the problems in our school."

"But I thought cards were banned," Matt said.

Mr. Leon turned to Matt. "Yes, Matt. Cards *were* banned. But that was not a good solution. You were right. We need to give people jobs to do at recess. And games and activities. Starting with these cards."

"Wait a second," Tyler said. "Does that mean we can bring *Monster Zap* cards to school again?"

Mr. Leon nodded.

"Even the Gross Eyeballs?" Tyler asked.

"Yes, Tyler."

"That's awesome!" Tyler shouted.

"But that's not all," Mr. Leon said. He pointed to the flat roof of the school.

Everybody looked up. The caretakers were there, waving down to the students.

Tyler waved back. "I *knew* they liked to play games up there."

"Everybody stand back," Mr. Leon said.

The caretakers started to throw things off the roof. Down came Hula-Hoops, basketballs, footballs and soccer balls. They were raining down from the rooftop.

Tyler started jumping up and down and pointing at some small, rubber balls that bounced super high. "Look! My bouncy balls! They're back!"

Matt's eyes went wide. "Is that your science project, Tyler? How did that get up there?"

Tyler's face went red. "Uh, I have no idea."

By now the whole school was yelling and clapping.

Mr. Leon took the megaphone.

"We will make sure there are games and activities at recess time. Captain Cleanup promises that the schoolyard will be a fun, safe place for all!"

The noise was so loud that some people in the houses across the street opened their doors to see what was happening.

"Captain Cleanup! Captain Cleanup!" voices chanted in the schoolyard.

Mark walked over to Matt. "Uh, hey, Matt," he said. "Is it okay if Steve and I join the Super Squad?"

Matt looked down at their hands. Matt and Steve had already drawn pictures. But this time they weren't of Mr. Leon.

They were pictures of Matt and Steve as Blue-Fanged Gobblers.

Matt smiled. "Sure you can. Anyone can be in the Super Squad."

Steve and Mark high-fived each other, then joined in the cheering.

Mr. Leon turned to Matt. The noise was so loud, he leaned in close. "Look, Matt. Your idea inspired the whole school."

Matt nodded. Mr. Leon was right. Already Victoria and Emily had started skipping lessons. Tyler was bouncing his Super Ball against the wall. Everyone was coming together. Matt had never seen the students and teachers so excited about recess before.

"Your idea inspired me too, Matt. So I have something for you." Mr. Leon took something out of his pocket. Matt could see it was a card.

But not just any card. It was printed on shiny gold foil, like his favorite Blue-Fanged Gobbler card. But on this card there was a picture of Matt! The words *Super Squad* were on the card too.

"Wow!" Matt said. "You made that for me?"

"One more thing," Mr. Leon said. He handed Matt a blank card.

"What's this?"

"It's the most important card of all," Mr. Leon said.

"But it's one of your blank ones."

"Exactly," Mr. Leon said. "I need you to do something very, very important with it."

"What?" Matt asked.

Mr. Leon leaned in even closer. "Can you teach *me* how to draw a Blue-Fanged Gobbler?"

Matt's face broke into a huge grin. "As long as you don't ban it," he said.

ACKNOWLEDGMENTS

I owe a huge thanks to my wife, Danielle Saint-Onge, for all of her amazing ideas and support. You wouldn't be reading this book without her!

JEFF SZPIRGLAS has written several award-nominated nonfiction books and two terrifying novels for middle-grade readers, *Evil Eye* and *Sheldon Unger vs. the Dentures of Doom*. With his wife, Danielle Saint-Onge, he is the co-author of *Something's Fishy* and *Messy Miranda*. He's worked at CTV Television and was an editor at *Chirp*, *chickaDEE* and *Owl* magazines. He lives in Toronto with his twin children and two cats (the cats are not twins). In his spare time, he teaches grade two.